This book is dedicated to all those living in, or touched by,
the leaves, branches, or roots of a unique family tree.

With love to Nick and Sophie, I am so blessed to be given the gift of being your parent.

With thanks to my illustrator & friend, Erin Cahanes, for bringing these characters to life.

With thanks to Ron Deal, who is an inspiration on his mission to mend unique families.

With honor to my parents, who model love and perseverance in over sixty years of marriage.

With gratitude to my husband, Alistair, for his support, encouragement, & love on life's journey!

-Karen Jacques

ISBN 978-1-59298-863-1
Library of Congress Catalog Number: 2015908392
Printed in the United States of America
First Printing: 2015
19 18 17 16 15   5 4 3 2 1

Written by Karen Jacques
Illustrated & Designed by Erin Cahanes
Edited by Beaver's Pond Press, Inc.

BPP Beaver's Pond Press, Inc.
7108 Ohms Lane
Edina, MN 55439-2129
(952) 829-8818
www.BeaversPondPress.com

To order, visit www.ItascaBooks.com or call
(800) 901-3480. Reseller discounts available.

Unique Family Tree Productions, LLC ™

MONSTERS Have My BROTHER!

Author
Karen
Jacques

&

Illustrator
Erin
Cahanes

Something in **Sticky Alley's** not right.

My brother **Lemmy**
was just here last night.

But this morning he's not in this room or the *other*.

Could it be that monsters have taken my **BROTHER?**

Maybe Lemmy has left me a **clue!**

I've seen this before on **Shoo Bee Doo.**

I look under here
and check up
there . . .

and give a quick *hug*
to his teddy bear.

I say **HELLO** to his pet frog, Ned.

Then I check under the **bed**.

As I feel all around,
I find something kind of **round.**

MY FIRST CLUE!

I've seen this car before.

When it came to our house,
Lemmy ran to the door.

She's on the phone, as I try not to **cry** . . .

Then she hands it to me, "Dottie, Lemmy wants to say, *HI!*"

He's alive!

I grab for the phone with a yelp.

"Are you okay, Lemmy?
Do you need my **help?**"

Now that's really weird, and a little bit **scary.**

Why did he just call our **mom**
by name . . . **SHERRY?**

Wait!
Maybe **his home** is my
FINAL CLUE!

They always have
three clues on
Shoo Bee Doo.

But three clues later, I'm still in **suspense.**

This **mystery** just doesn't make any sense.

Maybe **Lemmy's** not
my big brother anymore.

HEY!
There he is, I see him
outside the door!

"LEMMY,
you're **here!**
How did you
get away?

Will the **monsters** be back, or do you get to stay?"

"MONSTERS?"

Lemmy says.

"Oh, **Dottie!** Let me explain.

Before you were born, I lived on **Swamp Lane.**"

"Then **Dad** moved to Sticky Alley, a few miles north.

I have two **homes** and I go back and forth.

"Even though you and I don't have the same **mother,**

wherever I am, I'm still your big **brother.**

Change is frightening and hard, it's true.

But without this change, I would not have **YOU!**"

Then we watch
Shoo Bee Doo,
and give **Ned** a snack.

And **Mom** makes
Spaghetti
because
Lemmy is back.

At bedtime, he
comes in to hug
me ***goodnight.***

You might live with Mom,
you might live with Pop.
Families blend together,
some might foster or adopt.
No matter what you call them,
a stepparent or a blended home.
They come in all sizes, that's how
UNIQUE FAMILIES are grown.

THE ROOTS OF UNIQUE FAMILY TREE PRODUCTIONS

KAREN JACQUES was inspired by her stepson Nick and her daughter Sophie to create the characters of Lemmy and Dottie. When Sophie wondered why her big brother wasn't always home, Karen thought the best way to explain the situation was through a book, but that book couldn't be found. On her mission to find a book with positive characters for her children to identify with, Karen learned that traditional families (both biological parents in the same home) are no longer the majority population of American homes. Approximately 70% of children living in America are living in unique family situations. Hence, Unique Family Tree Productions was born.

"Loving and learning to be me in my UNIQUE FAMILY TREE."

ERIN CAHANES is a graduate from the Art Institutes International Minnesota. Having a stepparent of her own has influenced Erin to bring life and love to the Monster family. Her college animation background has helped to infuse the illustrations with personality and emotion. Erin's connection to the overall message has driven her to make Lemmy and Dottie characters children can identify with, ultimately bringing a positive child-like perspective to life's difficult topics.